FRANCESCA CATLOW

One Corfu Summer

Nothing is perfect, even in paradise.

Gaia
Fenrir

I dedicate this novella to everyone who didn't like Nico in previous books. Enjoy.

Contents

Prologue: Nico – 2018

'Come on, little brother, I'll race you.' Kostas raised one of his thick eyebrows and looked at me with childish glee. He might not have been a child, but he could never help himself. Every Monday morning we would take our motorbikes out and find new places for adventure, new roads and new dirt tracks. Then, with less new roads to find, Kostas would sometimes push to ride through wilder terrain. I was happy to follow his lead. My reward was always a slice of sticky honey baklava on our way home. A tradition born many years ago when we were boys. Back when it was pushbikes we went about on, and a Saturday that we cycled. Now Mondays were our day off; time away from the family business, together. Time to enjoy the freedom of our twenties.

'Don't be a pussy, Nico.' Kostas's bike skidded beneath his laughter, his left foot firm in the ground as the bike kicked up dust towards me, encasing him in a cloud. He knew what he was doing. Always goading. Always with his elbow in my ribs and a cheeky grin. Two, three circles of dust then he was off down the track. I kicked my bike into action and followed him. I'm not a pussy and I wasn't going to let my older brother think it was so. I was happy to race him. The thought of Mama tutting, her hands glued on her hips, clouded my brain like the dust from the bike. If she knew where we were, it would be more than tutting about racing.

Kostas's shoulder-length hair whipped and lashed about with his bare back tense under the vibrations of the motor. All it took was one tyre to fail. Like the sun had lost its hold on the earth, Kostas lost control of the bike. The handlebars twisted and it all went left, the sleek white metal frame contorted as he rolled like a rag doll before his skull hit the olive tree.

My brakes were screeching to stop me. I was screaming to stop him. I couldn't recognise him. He wasn't my brother anymore. He was just burst skin and raw nerves and bones. Nothing was where it should be. Nothing was how it should be.

Alice – 2019

'Are you two seriously not ready yet?' Lottie's head poked in through the balcony door, eyeing us, Elli and me, under her metallic-blue eyeliner. The setting sun over her head gave her tightly pulled black ponytail a dark-red hue.

'Don't be like that, darling.' I did my best to soften my expression. Lottie was having girlfriend trouble. It was one of the reasons we decided to get away. We had seen each other, just not very much, as we all went to different universities. When Lottie found out her girlfriend had cheated on her, we decided to grab whatever last-minute deal we could find, and escape. That's how we ended up in Corfu. It was a quiet resort, but not too far from Sidari, and we thought it would be perfect just to sunbathe and forget about exam results or the opposite sex. Well, the same sex in Lottie's case.

'Since when do you say *darling* so much?' Lottie crossed her arms and lent on the white-plastic door frame.

'Oh yes,' Elli piped in, grinning at me in the mirror while applying her bronzer, 'I've noticed that too!'

'Do I? One of the girls on my course says it a lot.' I slipped on my slingback, strappy silver shoes and swept one hand in front of my body. 'Ready.' I announced.

'Thank god.' Lottie rolled her eyes. 'Let's eat. I'm bloody

starved.'

In minutes we were exploring, making our way along the main road through the resort of Agios Stefanos. Lottie still had a bit of a face on her, but I was sure the poor love was just hangry. She was looking a little thin and I was pleased we had a chance to feed her up. Both Elli and Lottie are much shorter than me, tiny little things. That's not to say I'm tall, although with Lottie wearing flip-flops and me in heels, there was a good few inches between us.

Everywhere smelt delicious, like summer barbecues and fresh peppers sprinkled with oregano. We were spoilt for choice and Elli decided we should follow the sound of traditional music in the not-too-far distance.

'Quickly, this way,' she said and darted across the road. Without hesitation, I followed her. The sound of a motorcycle coming up quickly made me skip a step across the road and my slingback shoe slipped off. There was no way I had any time to stop to grab it, so I quickly carried on, hoping I could get it once the bike was gone.

As I glanced over my shoulder, I saw the bike swerve around my shoe, the wheels snaking about the road before steadying, then pulling into a dusty car park to stop.

His helmet was off but his engine was left on as he marched towards us. It seemed as though his scowl was almost digging into his bones. I was scooping to pick up my shoe, ready to say *sygnómi*, the Greek for sorry. I knew about five words and that was one of them.

'Crazy girl!' he snapped, before I could speak. 'You nearly kill me!'

'Sorry.' Instinctively, it came out in English.

'She didn't lose a shoe just to piss you off, mate.' Lottie butted in. She and Elli were standing as tall as their tiny frames would let them, but it wasn't exactly intimidating. The man looked at us all and shook his head with an exasperated expression of disgust before a tssk sound vibrated out of him.

'Buy shoes that fit, crazy girl. You are dangerous.' Then he muttered in Greek under his breath.

'I'm sorry, okay? I didn't mean to. *Sygnómi*, yeah?' I called as he started walking to where he had left his bike. He turned back to face us and looked me over with fresh eyes before a line was carved deeper between his brows.

He left us with the words, 'You could have killed me. Or worse.'

When he had marched out of earshot, Elli looked over at Lottie and me, and said, 'What's worse than death?'

'Spending time with him. Grumpy sod,' Lottie quipped, before wrapping an arm around me. 'Don't worry about him. He was just being a moody prick. Let's get some dinner.'

'Bloody hell, at least grumpy sod had a helmet on. Look at him!' Elli nodded towards the sound of a bike coming up from behind me. Lottie and I turned to see a topless, fat, older gentleman on a comically small, rusty scooter … Face Timing. His bike slowly wobbling underneath him while he chatted away towards the phone in front of his face. No helmet. One hand on the handle bars. Face Timing. 'Now I know what he means by *worse than death*. You could've ended up with him on top of you.' She bit her lip like she'd said something terribly naughty, as Lottie spat with laughter. 'Come on.' Elli gently elbowed me in the ribs, and we turned to carry on walking with the horror of a very leathery fat man gently scooting past.

As the path narrowed, Elli slipped ahead then turned back to us, eyes wide as the sound of traditional music blared out of nearby speakers.

'Here.' She tilted her head towards the noise. 'We're going here.' Even Lottie looked practically giddy as the waiters found us a table next to the central walkway in the open terrace.

I couldn't help but feel residual tension from the conflict. I would never intentionally hurt anyone, and I wouldn't just leave a shoe in the middle of the road. I told myself to push it to one side, but my stomach felt as tightly squeezed as fresh juice.

I focused on the fact we had been placed right next to the action. Greek dancing, men's legs flying in all directions. We took it all in. Clapping and laughing as we consumed juicy, fat olives on big Greek salads until I'm sure I smelled exclusively of fresh onions and feta. It all helped to ease the leftover adrenaline that was still making me a little unsteady.

After finishing our meals, Elli suggested finding a quiet bar. She gave me a little look, a lift of her eyebrow. Her round, dark eyes did their best to send me messages before she turned and was engulfed by her thick cloak of naturally blonde hair. I would absolutely kill to look like either of them. Lottie's half-Chinese with the most amazing long, straight hair and light golden skin. Elli has the darkest doll eyes that contrast her icy skin and hair. Both were and are stunning. They tan beautifully too. Unlike me. Being a redhead, I feel lucky if I get freckles and a burnt nose.

It was still early in the evening, which meant the bars weren't overcrowded yet. It was a sweaty July and the resort was clearly a popular one, but it was still quite small and not too overflowing.

Elli started pointing towards a place with wicker tables with glass tops and only a few were taken. We were soon settled with drinks menus, ready to consume cocktails and talk to Lottie about the cheating incident. She hadn't told us much at all, only that Tess had cheated on her and that she didn't want to talk about it. We didn't even know if they were still together or how she found out. Every time we asked about it, she diverted with topics she knew would catch us out. For me, it was Ethan.

Ethan was in the same uni halls as me, his room directly above mine. I wouldn't say I was obsessed with him – that would be creepy – but I did find him to be rather gorgeous. Other than a few flirtations on the stairs, we rarely saw each other, and now we were going into different houses, I wasn't sure I'd see him much at all. Perhaps in the union. Sometimes I would see him there.

The sound of shattering glass cut through my thoughts and everyone in the bar snapped to look where it had come from. A table a few along shouted, '*Opa!*' and cheered. The man apologising to his boss for dropping a bottle of booze was athletic with charming messy hair. His tight black jeans and fitted white shirt were crisp and neat, in contrast to the shaggy mocha hair that perfectly framed his eyes. Sadly, this was the same man whose bike had nearly tripped over my shoe. He had already spied us, of course. Maybe we were the reason for the bottle being dropped. Either way, he pasted on an obligatory thin smile for the occasion; the aniseed smell of ouzo pricked the air as he did his best to clear up the mess before making his way over to us.

'What can I get you to drink?' We all looked up at him standing over us with a pencil hovering over a tiny notepad.

I opened my mouth but Lottie jumped in with her order in a burst of cold, curt words, sharply followed by Elli. As though their drinks orders were somehow loaded with venom. When it got to me, I'd completely forgotten what I'd wanted. Flustered,

I just passed him my menu and said, 'You can decide.'

'That's not like you.' Elli's eyebrows lowered, narrowing her eyes at me.

'I can't pick.' I turned back to the waiter. 'You seem to know everything. You decide.' I could hear Lottie sniggering behind me. 'We're on holiday. I don't want to make any decisions that might accidentally leave me without any shoes.' The waiter scowled and his hand holding the pencil fell slack.

'No, no, you pick. Your drink, you pick.' His firm tone crawled along my skin like an irritating rash.

'No. I'm the customer and I want you to surprise me.' I'm not sure what had come over me. The juxtaposition of being pissed off with someone so attractive, perhaps? Or maybe all that adrenaline had stored itself away, ready to pounce on him? I couldn't really explain it other than I thought he had been disproportionately rude to me and it was my turn to give it right back.

'As you like. Thank you very mutz,' he said. His jaw was tense but he smiled before he made his way back towards the bar. Glancing over my shoulder, I noticed the older gentleman behind was instantly telling the waiter something and pointing at bottles. As I realised what I had done – giving someone else complete control over my drink – I felt utterly silly. What if he picked something I hated? In fact, I would be lucky if I didn't end up with spit in my drink after that. I would still have to pay for it and politely drink it.

'Well'— Elli tilted her head to the side, 'there's definitely some heat between you two. Cool accent too.'

I almost spat with indignation as Lottie chuckled at my side. 'What a pointless waste of hot anger,' Lottie began. 'I don't think Alice is capable of hate sex.'

8

From there, Elli and Lottie were chatting but I couldn't concentrate for fear of what I might get to drink. Some really alcoholic concoction, and then look like the idiot who couldn't handle her drink? I should have ordered something simple with gin or schnapps and just been polite to him.

When the puppy-eyed waiter came back to our table, he was holding a silver tray with a bowl of nuts and three tall glasses with sparklers glittering out of them.

'Sexy Greek,' he said, placing an orange drink in front of Elli, who blushed when it was handed to her. 'Tequila sunrise,' he added, handing over Lottie's choice. 'And for the girl who does not know what she likes or how to walk over roads, gin fizz.'

'Bloody hell, your favourite, Alice!' Elli sounded genuinely taken aback, but that was the moment where our eyes locked together. Mine and his. The big, dark eyes of the man before me. Half of his face lifted into an arrogant smile that was peeping over what was left of his irritation for me – obviously pleased with himself that he could indeed pick me out what I wanted, and did apparently know everything. 'For the beautiful, crazy girl, Alice.' And then he was gone, making his way back to the bar.

'To be fair, Alice, if you could manage angry sex, I bet he would be good at it,' Elli mused as she watched him walk away.

Lottie had decided she was too tired from travelling, and so we left after one drink. I might have pushed the decision along a little myself. I could feel the heat of his eyes on the back of my neck and I found it unbearable. Elli and I both knew Lottie's reason for wanting to leave early: it was to divert attention from any conversation about her. When our whispers about the waiter had dwindled, she could likely sense our focus beginning to shift. Not that we said that, of course. We just shared little looks when Lottie jumped up to pay at the bar. Although, I was just relieved to be leaving.

A Short Walk

After a day or two lounging next to the pool, we loaded up with beach bags bursting with towels and drinks, then marched down towards the sea. Our flip-flops made our arrival known to everyone before we were in sight, right up until our feet met the sand. The soft golden grains formed a cushion for our feet and our noise.

Rows of sunbeds and parasols overlooked the Mediterranean. I pushed my sunglasses up my nose a little more to protect my eyes from the glare of the sun skimming the sea. Sadly, as poor students, we had to skip the sunbeds to save our money for nights out and food so we kept on marching to the edge of the water where we placed our towels for the day.

'I'm going in,' Lottie announced. She slipped off her flip-flops and was already set. She had made her way down in her high-leg black swimsuit and nothing more. She had the attention of a young chap, who I think was hoping we would use his sunbeds. Not that Lottie noticed or cared, of course.

'Oh, not yet, darling. Let's warm up a bit first.' I smiled and dipped my wide-brimmed straw hat, then shimmied out of my beach dress to lie on my towel.

'Elli?' She tilted her head, almost scowling at her with her hands firmly pressed to her hips.

'Maybe in a bit. I've only just put lotion on.' Elli pressed her lips together into a smile and shrugged as she settled herself on the towel next to me. Lottie rolled her eyes at us and stormed off into the shallow water, going quite a way before actually starting to swim. Unlike me, Lottie was a very strong swimmer and used to compete when she was little.

'What are we going to do?' Elli hissed at me, lifting her weight onto one arm. Lottie was far enough away not to hear us, but we both hissed just in case.

'Oh gosh, I'm not sure. She's like an overboiled egg.'

'What?' Elli scoffed.

'Oh I don't know, darling. She's hard to crack and all that. If we push her too hard, she'll just get worse.'

Elli slumped back down in a heap on her bright yellow towel then pressed her hand over her eyes to shade them. 'Bugger, bugger, bugger. We need a plan, Alice. She's clearly going through some stuff. Did you see how thin her legs are getting? I'm worried about her.'

I had noticed. Of course, I had. They'd gone a little bit past starving-student levels and more into control eating. We both agreed that at least she had eaten all her dinner, but had also noticed that nothing but coffee had passed her lips that morning. The plan was hatched that we'd both try to get alone-time with her, that perhaps having both of us staring at her wasn't working. Lottie never really liked to open up and I think I'd only seen her cry twice at that point, and both times were because beloved pets had died. Elli and I have cried thousands of times together. Mostly as Lottie rolled her eyes or told us jokes to cheer us up. My gosh, we had even cried when One Direction announced there was to be no more. That seems a little ridiculous now but hey-ho.

I was going to get Lottie to go to the shops with me, and see if I could infiltrate her that way. Elli was going to ask her to keep her company on a walk along the beach to decide where to go for lunch.

A few hours later and off they went, marching down the beach. I could only hope Elli would get something out of her so we could start the process of healing with her. They were gone for half an hour. I knew they'd be looking at menu boards and chatting to people along the beach. Then, after a place was chosen and I'd joined them for lunch, it was my turn.

'Right, I think I'm going to walk off lunch by looking about the shops. Who's with me?' Elli was quick to come up with an excuse, as I knew she would, so then it was down to Lottie.

'I think I might have a little nap.' Lottie picked up her phone from the table where our plates were being cleared away and the smell of the remains of a garlic-laden tzatziki was whisked away too.

'Oh, come on, it'll be nice.' My eyes darted from Elli to Lottie, hoping somehow Elli would pipe up and save me. Standing behind Lottie and tugging her bag up onto her shoulder, all she had for me was a grimace and a shrug. 'Oh please, someone come with me. It'll be nice to explore.'

'Go on your own and report back to us what's good.' Lottie was barely looking at me as she scrolled on her phone.

'Oh, no, maybe I'll go later in that case.' I started to think I should have waited until we had got back down to the beach and wondered whether trying again later would work.

'Don't be like that. If you want to explore then go and explore. I went in the sea when you didn't want to.' It was then that I realised she would think I was being childish if I didn't go. Her perfectly brushed eyebrow was lifted and her top lip was starting to curl. If I didn't go, she would question the whole thing. I'm not one to worry about doing things on my own, which might've made Lottie realise our plan to single her out.

'Okay, if you're sure you don't want to come … okay, well. I won't be long.'

I'd seen a little church on the way into the village. I decided to make my way in that direction and, if there wasn't anything else on the way, at least I could have a look inside and it would be just enough time to not arouse suspicion.

So, off I went. I'd left everything except my phone, purse and sunglasses at the beach. With the rays of the sun boring down on my head, I was already missing my hat. I smoothed my hair down where it was tightly pulled into a low bun, then tugged my fingers through my fringe hoping I didn't have hat-hair. Luckily, there were quite a few little shops selling clothes, toys and tourist essentials. I decided to pop into the next one to see if there was a mirror to at least check my hair. After about five minutes looking at postcards I decided I could probably make my way back to the beach.

'It's crazy girl, Alice.' I looked up to see the man from the night before smoking a cigarette, standing in the dusty little car park next to where I'd lost my shoe. It was right next to the clothing shop I'd just stepped out of.

'Oh, it's you.' My heart was suddenly more alive in my chest at the sight of him. His dark, olive skin and soft-looking hair tangled with the irritation of calling me crazy. I started to walk past him but he tapped his chest with the cigarette hand.

'Nico,' he announced, before discarding the little burning stick entirely to the dirt. Although, he did carefully stamp it out as he reached forward to shake my hand.

'Alice.' Of course, as soon as I said my name, I realised he already knew it. A smile crossed his full, Greek lips as I felt a pinch of annoyance at making myself look silly again.

'Yes, Alice. Have you been here in San Stefanos before?' he said.

'San Stefanos? I thought it was Agios Stefanos?'

He laughed and shrugged. 'Different companies call it different names. Same place.'

'Oh, well, no actually, I haven't. This is my first time in Greece. Anyway, I should be getting on.' I moved to leave once more but he stepped in time with me.

'I am sorry, yes? It was a bad day for me. Bad timing and I was rude.'

I still felt unsure of him, but at least he had the decency to apologise. In doing so, he had trapped me in my British desire to fall-in and be polite. I nodded and accepted but still let myself remark that I wasn't crazy. I lost a shoe. There was nothing crazy about a shoe slipping off. It wasn't an intentional act. There was a pause where he seemed to look me over, finishing on my flip-flops.

'Always buy shoes that fit you. Then you will have less accidents.' In all fairness, he wasn't wrong. Those shoes were a little bit big for me but the shop had a sale and I could only get them in a half-size too big. I didn't tell him that. I didn't want to validate his already sound-but-irritating observation. 'So, first time in Corfu. How do you like it?'

'It's beautiful and the people have all been so helpful.' I took a breath and looked at him right in the eye before adding, 'Well, most people.' He laughed at this, completely unfazed by the remark. 'Can you suggest where's nice to go?'

'I am new here too. But,' he said, looking about as though he were going to tell me a secret no one else should hear and leant closer to me, 'this is Corfu. All is nice.' His smile widened, revealing his perfectly straight teeth.

Even with his charming smile, I took this as a good excuse to exit the painful conversation at last. He was clearly local and worked locally. To say he didn't know anything locally made it clear that he was still of a mind to wind me up. I politely thanked him for his time and went to step away.

'No, no, I am new to the village. I come in from Sidari to work.' Something about his face softened. The muscles around his eyes relaxed as he took a breath to consider his words. My hand found my hip as impatience drew me in. 'Tomorrow,' he said, 'I will show you a beautiful bay.' His complete change-around made my words dry up and I found it hard to swallow.

'I can't leave my friends. I'm so sorry.' I hesitated, twisting my phone between my palms.

'Hire quad bikes. Meet me here, in the morning. Nine?' He started to walk away, back towards where we had seen him working the night before.

'I don't even know you ... and you call *me* crazy.'

'If you are here, we can go. If you're not ...' He raised his shoulders into a final shrug and he was off, walking back down past the shops.

Nico. I had gained his name and a belly full of confusion. Nico.

Lovey

Arriving back on the beach brought a barrage of questions at the mention of my new-found frenemy, Nico. Lottie couldn't stop laughing and Elli couldn't stop asking questions.

'Did you get his number?' she asked, kneeling on her towel and almost bouncing on her heels. I shook my head and wrinkled my nose at the thought of giving him the satisfaction of asking for his number. Elli was single too, since breaking up with her high school boyfriend around Easter. Well, he actually broke up with her but she seemed relieved if anything, as they never really saw each other. I just don't think Elli likes to disappoint or hurt anyone. I can't imagine her breaking up with anyone. She's also very good at burying her head in the sand. Not quite in the way Lottie does. Elli is more likely to go along with things for a quiet life and Lottie can't talk about her feelings.

'Well—' Lottie began. The mischievous way the late afternoon sun was glinting in her eye already had me worried. 'We have to go to that bar tonight, don't we, Elli? I'm positively parched thinking about it.' Then they were both in fits of giggles and I was regretting telling them anything at all.

Getting ready that night was frustrating at best. Even taking a moment to pick out clothes, or choosing between lip stain or lipstick, was met with one of the girls asking if I thought Nico would like it. However many times I told them I didn't even like him and that he came across as an arrogant, rude idiot, they just laughed. In fact, it seemed to be a catalyst for more laughing. On our way back from the beach, they had marched at a pace and gone straight to the quad bike hire to make enquiries for the next morning. When I protested, Lottie had announced that she would tell us all about Tess if I stopped moaning and enjoyed myself a little. Which was the one card she had to play to get me to go along with it all, hoping, of course, that Nico wasn't in fact a serial killer. I still refused to hire a quad bike though, although I did agree to go on the back of Lottie's if we did go in the morning.

I straightened my hair, leaving it loose, the dark, red threads complementing the freckles that were beginning to happily rest on my cheeks and shoulders.

'You look beautiful, Alice.' Elli appeared behind me in the mirror with a contented smile under her sweet turned-up nose.

'Thank you, darling. Although, I'll wait to see if I get praised by the lesbian in the room to be on the safe side.' At this, Lottie looked up from the bed where she was scrolling on her phone. Her eyes glanced at my lacy, white dress and she nodded.

'I'd do you.' Her tone was completely neutral and then she went back to her phone. This was Lottie's standard silly response.

'Perfect then. We're ready.'

It wasn't long until we had found another delicious taverna where we all had moussaka with aubergines topped with lashings of cheese sauce. This is when we settled in for Lottie to tell us everything about Tess, only to be told that, no, this wasn't the time or the place. If she was going to tell us anything, we had to first be at the bar where Nico worked and have had a few drinks. Then, and only then, would she tell us. Being a good friend takes priority over seeming like a stalker to a man I didn't care for, so in actuality, I had no choice in the matter.

When we sat ourselves at the same table at Nico's place of work, he was nowhere to be seen. A young woman came over to take our order, the same as the night before. Relief was an understatement. I hadn't realised how tense my body had been since Lottie had announced we had to go back to the same bar. Seeing it free of Nico left my shoulders with the freedom to relax a little.

Three drinks in and Lottie had no more excuses to make. She had to tell us what really happened with Tess. Apparently, she had picked up Tess's phone to look at the time and saw a message on there from a boy on her uni course. Basically, he was asking when he could see her again. She confronted Tess in a sensible, grown-up way and it all seemed like a suitable stream of answers. But Lottie was still left unsure.

'I wanted to believe her but something niggled away at me. There was this day where she cancelled on me, saying she was ill and all that'—Lottie took a deep gulp of her cocktail before continuing—, 'I knew it was crap.'

Reaching forward she grabbed a handful of nuts from the bowl on the table and stuffed them into her mouth. It was then that Nico caught my eye, serving a table to my left. I don't think the girls noticed and luckily Lottie carried on uninterrupted. I did my best to focus on her and forget that he was anywhere nearby.

'She had turned off my ability to find her on my phone. It just confirmed it all. I went to her house and her flatmate said she'd gone out. I knew where the boy lived. I Snapchatted her a picture of her car outside his place and she hasn't spoken to me since. She opened the Snapchat and didn't reply. After five months together, she just ghosted me. I called and texted but it was like we were never together.' Looking into her glass and rolling it between her hands, she added under her breath, 'I've seen them together, holding hands. Never trust a bisexual.' At this she shook her head a little and, in doing so, caught sight of Nico. It was worth it to see her sharp cheekbones lift as she leant forward to whisper, 'Your new boyfriend is here.' I turned to Elli, who was biting her lip to hold back her giggles. I rolled my eyes and decided to ignore their childish suggestions, instead staying on topic.

'I can't believe she ghosted you. That's absolutely—'

'Hey! The crazy girl table is here. Are you ready for tomorrow? Alice has said? Yes? We are out for an adventure.'

I could smell the sweet tang of Nico's aftershave on the breeze as he squatted down between Elli and me. It occurred to me that perhaps he was friendly and trying to make it up to me by making a joke out of it all, but I wasn't sure I trusted him. He looked equally between us all, smiling the way a friend would. We had already made our way through a couple of cocktails and the warmth I was feeling wasn't just the night breeze. A light numbness was washing over me.

The girls were an equal mix of sarcasm and excitement – chatting at Nico, asking him questions about where he was taking us and if we should trust him after the other night. I think they saw it as a cheap excursion with a handsome, private tour guide. After a moment more, he left to get us another round of drinks.

When he returned, he placed each drink down, complete with

sparklers, and then pulled a scrap of paper from his pocket and placed it in front of me on the table.

'My number. In case you have any problems.' He smiled at me then went back to continue his work. I scooped up the number and typed it into my phone, ignoring all the eyebrow wiggles and comments from my friends.

'I'm so happy you're getting a holiday boyfriend, Alice. You could have any man in the whole wide world and all you've done for the past year is obsess over the boy who lives above you.' Elli looked across at me before sipping at her three straws. In my drunken haze, I thought I must tell Nico he shouldn't be using plastic straws, and most certainly not three.

'Don't forget, he had a girlfriend for about half of that,' Lottie said while pulling her tube top back up a little.

'Yes, yes,' I interrupted. 'Two things, though. One, I don't have a holiday boyfriend. I'm still not even sure I like him as a passing friend. And two, I didn't tell you ... Ethan and I spoke the other day at an end-of-year house party thing. I mean actually spoke for maybe an hour. I didn't mention it because I didn't want to get my hopes up.'

'If after an hour of talking to you he hasn't offered himself up on a big, fat plate, he isn't worth it.' Lottie waved her finger a little as she spoke. The bar had started to fill with happy holiday makers laughing and drinking. All were enjoying the residual heat left over from the sun and the sound of music that flooded the bar and the street beyond.

As our blood alcohol levels went up again, so did our laughter. Lottie visibly relaxed after telling us about Tess. I think being completely ignored and deleted was really hard for her. It would be for anyone. We had met Tess only once, when Elli and I went to visit Lottie for her birthday. They seemed really good together.

It was nice to relax with my friends again. To be together after our year away from each other. We had been friends for such a long time, I couldn't ever imagine being without them. Just the idea made me feel all teary and, quickly, Elli caught onto my strand of thinking.

'Oh shit, Alice is drunk. Look, look at her. Her eyes are misting up.' Elli tapped Lottie's leg repeatedly as I started to wave my hands in front of my eyes to prevent ruining my make-up.

'I just love you both so much. That's not a dreadful thing to say now, is it?'

'No, you just always say it when you're pissed.' Lottie waved her hand and Nico appeared by my side before squatting down next to me.

'More drinks?' He looked right at me and the urge to kiss him felt so intense that even though I didn't want another drink, I said yes just to get him out of my sight. Kiss him? I couldn't believe that tipsy me was so shallow that I could be swayed by his puppy eyes instead of focusing on the fact he kept calling me crazy. It was getting late and people were starting to head back to their apartments or hotels.

This time, Nico brought back four drinks. 'Nico, I don't think you can count, love.' Lottie pointed at the glasses.

'The boss said I did well tonight. No breaking things today. So, I am here, finished with a lemonade. Can I?' We all agreed, although I didn't really want him to. The way he made me feel like my clothes had been set on fire was beyond disconcerting.

He pulled a packet of cigarettes out of his back pocket and offered them about, but none of us took one. With that, he checked we didn't mind and smoothly lit one. Smoking isn't cool, but if it was, he would make it cool. I slightly envied that silly, little tobacco stick being taken in his mouth. I realised I was watching him and biting my bottom lip; my centre felt as hot as the tip of his burning cigarette. No matter how much I focused on what a prick he had been, his olive skin and messy hair were doing something to me that pushed out Ethan completely.

'So, how long have you worked here?' It might not have been the most groundbreaking question, but I was two steps past tipsy and desperate to make conversation that didn't involve me accidentally saying I wanted to kiss him.

He held up four fingers. 'Four nights.'

'Wait,' Lottie laughed, 'you broke a bottle of booze on your first shift and they let you come back?'

Nico nodded, the cigarette hanging out of the corner of his mouth as a puff of smoke appeared from his nose. 'I was being distracted. Not my fault. The owner is nice. He understands.'

'Where did you work before?'

He didn't answer me. He shook his head and said, 'No, no. Tell me about you.' He waved his hand across us all. 'Where are you from?'

We told him how we were all at different universities but we actually came from a county called Suffolk. Unsurprisingly, he hadn't heard of it. He then asked us how long we were staying, although that one felt more aimed at me. But I was doing my best just to be straight in my chair and not lean forward to press my fingers against his velvety-looking skin on his cheek, or tug at the buttons on his clean, white shirt to see what was underneath.

'Ten days. Well, we're here for six more days now.' Our eyes met for a silent moment that was just a touch longer than socially acceptable. I could feel the heat of it resting on my skin.

'Right'—Lottie slapped her bare thighs and stood up—'I'm going to need yet another wee soon, so I think it's time to stumble back to the apartment.' Elli and I began to pick up our phones and bits as Nico turned to me. 'You are not finished.' He pointed at my half-full glass. 'I can walk you back if you want to finish.'

'Nope!' Elli grabbed my arm and started pulling me around the table. 'She will see you for our adventure in the morning. This skinny beauty has had enough.'

I did my best to agree and protest simultaneously. I wanted to stay and look at him for just a little bit longer but I didn't want to admit to anyone how much I wanted to stay. It was dreadful to even admit it to myself. 'Okay, okay then, darling. Tomorrow, tomorrow.' I blew a kiss. It was meant to come across as casual but I'm quite sure I missed that mark too. Then the words that will forever haunt me passed my lips. 'Lovey-love-kiss!'

I turned and marched arm-in-arm with my two best friends as Elli squirmed, laughing so hard she complained she might wet herself, and Lottie kept saying in a silly, almost Shakespearean voice, 'Lovey-love-kiss!'

Why couldn't I have just said goodnight like a normal person? I was mortified but luckily drunk enough to laugh about it.

White Pebbles

'Sorry I am making you wait. My mama, she … it is long story.'
He looked at the quad bikes. 'Who is not riding?' I put my
hand up, which instantly made Nico tut and waggle his finger
towards me. 'No, no,' he said. 'Not you, lovey-love? You'll
have to come with me in this case. Come on.' As soon as he
said *lovey-love*, mortification rippled over my body again, right
to my toes. He edged forwards on his bike and adjusted his
backpack to put it on the front of his body. I turned to look
at my friends but they were practically giddy as I awkwardly
shuffled on, adjusting my shorts.

Then me and my dehydrated body were pressed to Nico. My
stomach felt a little queasy at first and I couldn't tell if it was the
excitement of having a legitimate reason to hold this handsome
stranger, or the gin from the night before. I let the air whip
around me, cooling my limbs, and I pressed myself to the heat
penetrating through his black sleeveless T-shirt. After a little
while I wanted to press my face to him, to feel the skin of his
shoulder against me but I knew the girls were right there behind
us on their quad bikes and there was no way I was going to give
them more reasons to poke fun. Plus, it's not that easy with a
helmet on.

The views across Corfu were breathtaking. We had seen a

25

fair bit on the coach when we arrived but there was something different about seeing it from a motorcycle. The feeling of being in among the olive trees and the raw sensation of having the fresh air on my skin instead of air-con. Soon we were able to look over everything. To my left, past the edge of the road was an expanse of trees and little houses dotted here and there. Then the turquoise Mediterranean Sea faded perfectly into the line of the sky. The endless blues were mesmerising.

After almost an hour on the bike, we stopped and followed Nico down a dirt path through a wood. It was so loud with insects and yet utterly peaceful. Not much was said as we made our way along. Early on Elli commented that it would be the perfect place to bring us to murder us, and her joke had left Lottie and me on edge. It did seem to be the perfect place. It wasn't until a fit-looking older couple strode past us going the opposite way that we relaxed a little. We relaxed enough to manage the odd question, or reflection on the beauty we were marching through. But that was all that passed our lips. Well, that and lots of water.

Here and there, attached to the trees along the path were signs that read LIMNI and how far it was to the beach. They were all hand-calved and something about them made it seem mysterious and even more like an adventure. We made our way down old stone steps, through more trees, until white pebbles were in view. It was the most incredible double bay with clear sea surrounded by craggy rocks and tall, pointed cypress trees. On both sides of the strip of stones, water gently lapped, rocking and cradling the people who found themselves on the narrow beach.

'Wow.' I breathed, looking across to the green, rocky mound opposite and the incredible glittering sea in front of me. It was

26

attached by a small pebble beach.

'I am glad it is good.' Nico looked across to me and smiled. He wasn't that much taller than me, maybe a few inches when I wasn't in heels. Lottie was past us and pulling off her black swing dress over her head and running into the sea without saying a word, not that I could blame her. The midday sun was almost upon us and I was dripping before I came close to the sea. I opened my mouth to say something to Nico only for his phone to ring. Elli grabbed my arm.

'Come on, we have a moment. Thank god Lottie opened up a bit at last. I think you and Nico are a fun distraction too. It's nice to see you actually interacting with someone.'

'I do interact with people.'

'Don't pout. I'm only going off what you tell us, Alice. I'm not there to witness you and Ethan first-hand now, am I?' She was right though. Right about it all, really.

'That was my friend Harry. He is free today. He is English like you. I hope you don't mind – I invited him to join in.' Nico was at my elbow as we slipped off our shoes to paddle and watch Lottie splash about in the sea and shout at us to all get in.

'Oh really?' I shot a look at Elli who blushed without even thinking. Nico caught the exchange and quickly diverted it.

'He will bring his girl too, Maria. I can call and say no? If you like?' His eyes were a little panicked under his mop of hair but I did my best to share a reassuring smile. It would be nice to meet more people after all. Nico went on to drop his bag on the stones. 'I bring these.' He pulled out two snorkels with masks. A scream came from the sea making all our heads whip towards the noise.

It was Lottie. She then followed the scream with, 'Yes! Good one!' and came charging back out of the water. 'How many did you bring?'

'Two. You take them first. I have been many times before.' Nico passed them to her and I knew this was my chance to grab the opportunity to get to know him. Not that I would have even admitted that to myself at the time.

'Elli, why don't you go with Lottie? I don't mind waiting. I might just paddle for now.' Elli didn't have to be told. She knew me better than I knew myself. It wasn't as though I was ditching them, in fact, my new friend was just creating a whole new adventure for us all.

Nico pointed the girls in the right direction, and off they went to explore, leaving us alone on the beach. Well, not actually alone. But away from anyone else to talk to but each other.

'It's a hot day,' Nico said as he slipped off his top in one swift motion and tossed it onto the round, white pebbles next to his bag. He then took three strides into the water and sat down, there in the shallow water's edge, the rise and the fall of the sea licking around him. 'Come,' he said looking up at me. 'The water is magic.'

So, I did. I slipped off my shorts and T-shirt, replaced my hat on my head, and glided into the water next to him.

'Why is the water magic?' I gave him a coy look under my wide hat.

'The sea is all magic. The sea takes pain and feels none of it.' He then paused, picking up a pebble from the sea bed then throwing it a short distance in front of us, making a hollow plop before it disappeared. 'That is what my mother says.'

Our conversation flowed naturally in a way that it only can for two strangers, because they know nothing of each other. So, everything is a new secret to be delivered. It was after a short while I realised – he was keeping me busy with questions and I wasn't managing to get many answers at all.

'So, Nico, if you live in Sidari, why do you work in Agios Stefanos? I would've thought there was plenty of work in Sidari? It's a small town isn't it?'

He had picked up another stone to throw, but this time he rolled it between his slender fingers. 'Before, I worked in the family business. It did not work out. My father, he closes it down. No more business, no more job. I want to find my own way. Get my own job away from my family.' Instead of throwing the stone, he dropped it back to where he had found it.

'Hey, Nico! Who is the redhead?' A girl's voice called across the stones. I turned to see a busty blonde with bright, pink lips marching along the pebbles hand-in-hand with a man with a mop of curly hair.

Nico stood and put his hand out to help me up. 'This is Alice. Maria and Harry.' He pointed over at them. And that was that. Maria started chatting to me straight away – telling me how she was half-English on her mother's side, asking me where I got my bikini from, and then, when Elli and Lottie came back, she was included into our fold like an instant friend. Nico had asked them to bring a picnic and more snorkels which was met with a ripple of praise from me and my girls. We sat about chatting and eating pita breads, olives and crisps, and honestly, in that moment I felt like doing exactly what Harry told us he had done. The year before, he came on holiday, met Maria and didn't want to leave. They seemed happy enough. Maybe I could shock the world and not be the forever-good girl and just move to another country.

I was daydreaming and looking over at Nico. He caught my eye and, in an instant, we were both just smiling across. Then his expression changed and a sharp word that I didn't understand spat out of his mouth. I thought perhaps he was in pain or suddenly angry but then he was up and sprinting. We all just watched him, completely puzzled. I even looked over to Harry for some kind of answer or reassurance but he just shrugged.

White pebbles kicked up from his bare feet, then water, as he ran towards the rocks at the edge of the bay. He plunged his hands into the depths of the water and pulled out a child.

An Accident

A little girl had been happily playing on the rocks. She was maybe four years old. Her mum's phone was ringing and she had run back to her towel to answer it. In that short space of time the girl slipped, caught herself on the rocks, and had gone under. Her mum couldn't stop thanking Nico and kissing him on the cheeks. Although the little girl seemed fine, she did have a bit of a bump on her head, and the mother left to take her to be checked over.

'Wow, Nico. Do you have any sisters that happen to be gay?' Lottie laughed. 'You're a proper charmer. Snorkels, getting your nice mates to bring food, and now you're a hero.'

'No, sorry. No sisters.' Nico laughed along with her, clearly enjoying the compliment.

'A brother then? For Elli?'

As Elli's cheeks raged scarlet and she hit Lottie's knee, Nico just shook his head. A smile remained on his lips, but his eyes lost direct focus. Suddenly he was more interested in what was in the distance than what was in front of him. Grabbing for his bag, he pulled out a packet of cigarettes, placed one in his mouth, and then tossed the pack at Harry. He took one, before offering them about.

I watched Nico from the corner of my eye. The sea breeze

suddenly felt as though the salt in the air had dried out the conversation and fluidity of before. Silently, smoke from Nico and Harry circled us leaving us waiting in a tense cloud.

As soon as Nico was finished with the cigarette, he quickly snatched up the snorkels and made some remark about how he was going to take a turn. Smiling across at us all, he then disappeared into the sea.

'Did I do something wrong?' Lottie's face looked like that of a young child who's lost their new toy. Maria and Harry looked at each other. Harry shrugged, running his fingers into his coiled hair and Maria sat forward pouting her pink lips.

'It's not your fault. Don't feel bad, girl, okay? Only, yeah, Nico has a brother. He was in a bike accident. Nico never talks about him. I only know because it was all over the local news when it happened. He has never told Harry about it. I was the one who told him. I don't know if Nico knows I know, let alone Harry. Anyway, that would be why he didn't like that question so much.' Maria's eyes seemed to turn an even more pale blue than before.

'I'm going to see if he's okay,' I announced, and grabbed the other set of snorkels. I could see him swimming further out. Picking my way into the water along the stones and rocks, I was soon swimming over to him.

Swimming past a shoal of striped fish, I grabbed at Nico's foot. He snatched it away and came straight out of the water where I met him. He looked me over under the steaming goggles and nodded towards a different edge of the bay, not far from the beach, but plenty far enough. We had to be careful; it was along the same strip where the girl fell in. Although that was very different, we were older and not distracted by looking for sea creatures, some of the rocks were sharp and it was a sensible idea to remain cautious. We found a rock to sit on while still being half-submerged. We took off our snorkelling gear and looked across to our friends taking up so much space on the small strip of beach. They were laughing and chatting while we were quiet. I didn't know whether to just come out and repeat what Maria had said. But then she had never told Nico she knew about his brother's accident. It might have been a bit much to tell him. Before I had time to decide, he took the choice out of my hands.

'I am sorry. I did not mean to be'—he waved his hands about, looking for the right words—'rude … again.' He pulled in a measured breath before continuing. 'Yes, I have a brother. Older than me. He, he was in an accident. He has problems now. With his head. He is more like a child than a man.'

He wasn't looking at me as he spoke but his eyes were reflecting the sun like highly polished steel.

'I'm so sorry, Nico. That's dreadful. I'm here if you want to talk about it.'

'No, no. You are on holiday you should be laughing with your friends not sitting on the sad rock with me.'

'But I want to sit on the sad rock with you. We wouldn't have even known about this place without you.' Instinctively, I put my hand over his under the water. His thumb carefully stroked my fingers that were resting next to it. It suddenly made sense to me: why he had been so upset at swerving around my shoe. Not only did he have the pressure of it being his first night in a new job, but his brother had suffered at the hands of a bike accident.

'I was with him. I watched him fall to the ground and I could do nothing.' Nico pulled his eyes away from the beach and met my gaze head on. 'I never talk about him. Why do I tell you this?'

I felt my face lift in a muddled pride at the idea that he could open up to me – me, the crazy girl. 'I'm so sorry. That's absolutely dreadful. What did you do?'

His eyes left mine, and under the water our hands began to mesh together more tightly. 'I call for help. They say he is lucky to live.' He shook his head and his top lip curled. 'No. It is not true. It would have been better to die.'

The stark words were so cold I could barely scrape together any words in return. All I managed was to whisper, 'Why?'

'He is worse than dead. He is a child now, maybe three or four, glued inside the face of a man. I would want to be dead. It is no life.' He let go of my hand and turned to face me on the rock, suddenly more animated and full of fire. 'Kostas was all big personality, fast bikes and parties. He was in love, too. I think he would have married her. She was crazy like him. He lived. He worked hard with my father for the shop but when he was not working, he was fun and … life. Living. Laughing, always.'

'And now?'

'Now? He throws his food if it is something he does not want, gets angry when we say no … The body of a man and the brain of a boy.'

I softly edged in more questions. Finding out that the year before, at only twenty-six, Kostas had a blowout tyre on a dirt track they were both riding along. The way he rolled off his bike had caused broken bones but saved him from an instant death. As his momentum slowed, he came to a stop when he hit his head on an olive tree. It was enough to cause swelling of the brain. They were in the middle of nowhere and it took too long to get the help that was needed. The wait for medical intervention caused permanent damage to his brain, and therefore his whole personality changed. He couldn't work or even be left to cook a meal alone. They had to shut the family business for Nico's mother to look after him full time.

'I needed to get work too. Everything in Sidari reminds me of him. Laughing with him, drinking with him, riding with him. I can't even eat baklava! It reminds me of who he was and hurts too much. So, I come to Agios Stefanos for work. I meet Harry and Maria through a friend a few months ago. Harry told me of a job and, on my first night, I meet you. Beautiful, crazy, Alice with the skin like clouds.' His hand came up to my face and his wet fingers lightly brushed my cheek.

I looked over at the beach; our friends weren't there anymore. 'I think everyone has gone snorkelling. I can't see anyone.' I hadn't noticed them, but then I was engrossed in listening to Nico. Lots of people were swimming and snorkelling, but I think all had decided to give us and our rock a wide berth.

'Come.' He started to wash out the mask of his snorkel. I copied before we both put them on, making our lips look like cartoon fish. Our eyes bulged a little under the pressure. Not that I cared what I looked like really. I just wanted to explore and have fun. Carefully pushing ourselves off the rock, we entered another world together.

I followed on next to him, constantly pointing at things for each other to share in. Bright-orange starfish with thick arms like fat sausages, then fish that were only obvious when viewed from their tall flat side but from the front were so slim, they almost vanished. In the clear waters of Corfu, everything was visible, and to my horror I saw how much I liked Nico. More than I'd felt for anyone in a long time. I saw past the angry tones of a few days before, and I was left looking at a man who was hurt, afraid and alone in equal measure.

Dreaming

'Are you ever going to get dressed?' Elli looked down at me. I was lying on my bed in the apartment, wrapped in a thin, white towel that was a little bit like cardboard, and I could feel heat resonating from my shoulders where the sun had left its memory of the day.

'Nope.'

'Come on, Alice. I'm bloody starving after today. Get your arse off the bed and get dressed,' Lottie said and plonked herself down on her bed to look over me. Reluctantly, I agreed. Nico wasn't working that evening and we planned to have a quiet and early night.

Of course, that's not what happened. Yes, I got up, dressed, we went out for food, but then we found ourselves drinking shots of ouzo with three ladies in their fifties who had been coming to the same place on holiday together for twenty years. They got us up dancing, telling us about everywhere to eat and drink – which was basically that everywhere was good. If we wanted to do any fabulous excursions, we should chat to San Stefano Travel where we could book lots of amazing things. One of which was boat trips: that went straight to the top of our to-do list for the morning. We shared all about our day snorkelling and exploring, and they decided that would be added to their list for the week.

'I think we're you lot in thirty years,' one of them laughed. I can't remember their names now. Only that we all laughed so much we cried and they had more energy than any of us. I hoped we would be like them in thirty years. Nothing would make me happier.

They all did shots and one of the trio announced it was time to dance again. In a whirl of floral skirts and painted lips, everyone was laughing and dancing. In my warm haze, holding hands with Elli shouting along to some music in the bar, I couldn't help but think of the moment Nico had placed his hand on my knee on the ride home. With the heat of the night, I could almost feel his fingers still lingering on me. Excusing myself, I went back to our table and slowly sipped at my drink.

I closed my eyes for a brief moment as a cool breeze rippled past. I couldn't really explain my attraction to him, other than the fact he was good-looking. It didn't feel that shallow though. I was sure there was more to discover, but I didn't know it. With Ethan, I knew he was smart as well as handsome. He had always been polite to me, holding doors open and such. Yes, there was the initial attraction aside from anything else, but with Nico, my first thought was how rude he was, so it seemed mad for me to like him so much. At least I had a little more understanding as to why he overreacted. If it had been my first day of work and someone had nearly made me come off a bike, I'd have probably been exactly the same. Thinking about it, he was quite restrained. Something about him lingered on my skin. The vulnerability under the surface seemed to be drawn out in my presence. Like a splinter in hot water, it just seemed to creep out of him. His strength in being there for his family pouring out of his open wound made him intriguing and hard to define. I wanted to be near him, so I picked my phone up and sent him a message:

We're drinking and dancing. You? xxx

Nico:

Nothing. Thinking about a girl. X

So, I told him to join us. Everyone was laughing and having fun, mixing together. What was one more person to the medley? I wasn't as drunk as the others, as they were two drinks ahead of me and I hadn't been interested in the shots. I just had that warm feeling from my toes to my chest. Although, it might have been the anticipation of seeing Nico again.

We had a table near the edge of an outside terrace and, while everyone danced and laughed, I kept an eye open for Nico. He pulled up right outside and left his bike on the road. He came towards me and we automatically put our arms around each other. His hands felt cool on my back. I was wearing a fitted crop T-shirt and a matching maroon maxi skirt.

'Crazy, beautiful Alice.' He whispered so close to my ear that it didn't matter about the loud music. I could feel the smile in his voice.

'Nico! What a coincidence seeing you here on your day off when you don't live here. Passing through?' Lottie grabbed both of our shoulders, steadying herself while Elli stood behind her, laughing.

'I missed you all, the crazy, sexy ladies.' Nico winked at her.

Lottie pretended to vomit on our feet before screaming, 'I love this song,' and turning to grab our new friends to get up again and dance. Before Elli went, I grabbed her hand.

'We might just go for a little walk. I've got my phone and tracking is on, so you can find me, before you say anything.'

Instead of saying anything, she just smiled and gave me a peck on the cheek. Turning back to Nico, I took in the picture of his good looks. I couldn't resist but to push his hair out of his coffee-coloured eyes. It was just as soft as I had imagined. He offered to buy me a drink and I offered to take him for a walk on the beach. His fingers found mine and soon we were walking towards the sea.

Starlounger

On our way along, I asked how his brother was. He still lived with his parents and helped out with his brother in any way he could. The answer was quite plain. Not defensive, but distinctly vague, so I didn't push him.

In return, he asked me about my family. I'd lived a charmed life by comparison to his past year. I have two sisters, both much older than me as I was an obvious accident. I've never been close to either of them and nothing bad has happened to them or any other family member of mine. Or anyone I'm close to, for that matter. I didn't put it like that, of course.

Walking along, I watched the moonlight dance on the waves. The sound of music from various bars travelled along in a mismatch of basslines. As we got closer to the sea, that was the sound that took over: the rhythmic lapping and crawling of the sea up onto the sand.

Nico grabbed hold of one of the sunbeds and dragged it so we could sit next to each other and look out to sea.

'Do you have a boyfriend? Back in England?'

I shook my head, surprised he would even think that. 'Why? Do you have a girlfriend?'

'No, no. Not for a couple of months anyway.' He cupped his hands around a cigarette to light it then threw the lighter on the ground along with everything else from his pockets. 'Even if I did, I would leave her for you. So, it is lucky there is no other girl.' Half his face lifted into a cheeky smile, only visible in outline from the distant electric lighting of the village that lined the beach from behind us and the glittering moonlight in front.

'That's a bit presumptuous, isn't it?'

'I don't know this one,' he said, before taking another lungful of smoke.

'Presumptuous? Oh … forward, over-confident.'

At this, Nico laughed out the smoke. He laughed so hard he began choking over it, spluttering and laughing simultaneously.

'You know you shouldn't smoke,' I said. 'It's bad for you.'

He made a little noise of agreement in the back of his throat as his laughter died down. 'I started after Kostas's accident. Life can be snatched too fast. I don't think mutz about the future now. It is good to laugh, though.'

I didn't continue to argue my point. It actually seemed a little pointless with everything he had been through. Instead, I silently took the cigarette out of his hand and put it out on the sand before placing it next to his lighter, determined to at least put the thing in the bin at some point so as not to litter. He rolled his eyes and a small, irritated pout pressed on his lip. Wanting to remove the expression, I leant forward and kissed him. The fresh, smoky tobacco taste was soon on my lips and in my mouth. Not unpleasant. His fingers moved over my back and pulled me in and onto his lap. My hands found the soft tendrils of his hair and gently gripped them, pulling him as close as I possibly could. It had been so long since I'd kissed anyone I felt so much passion for. I'd been on dates, but nothing that felt so raw and real. Then Nico slipped out of my grasp, almost gasping for air. He grabbed the sunbed again, adjusting it back to its original position while I was still sitting on it. I laughed, but I had a sinking feeling that this was a signal that the night had come to an abrupt end and that maybe he thought he should get home at such a late hour. Then I caught sight of the light in his eyes, the lift of his cheek bones and the intense way he made eye contact with me. Carefully, he laid me back and found my lips again before taking my waist in his hands and pulling me to the edge of the sunbed.

His soft, full lips made their way along my neck and I shivered against the stifling heat of the still, summer-night air. His eyelashes tickled at my collarbone before his hand found its way under my bra to cup my breast. 'You want this, yes?' he said in a low, breathy voice. I managed to agree while biting my lip, thinking about what was to come. My heart was racing with the adrenaline from excitement and the fear of getting caught.

Nico edged himself off the sunbed and carefully lifted my skirt to my knees before tenderly nibbling and kissing my legs, my thighs, and then he was completely engulfed by my skirt. At a glance, anyone could have mistaken me for being alone on the beach just watching the stars. Only, I was gripping the wooden frame of the lounger so hard I thought my fingernails might break and my breathing was quickly past the level of erratic. I tried to bite my lip to hold it all in, but the longer he was there, the harder it became to control. Every muscle in my body froze rigid, and beads of sweat from my skin were like tears of joy dripping down onto the sand before an uncontrollable gasp jumped from my lungs, leaving the stars above spinning around my head.

As Nico emerged from the depths of my skirt, I could hear a phone vibrating on the floor. Sweating and panting, I didn't move. I didn't care. But Nico passed it to me. It was my phone and a picture of Elli dressed as an elf from a Christmas party was on the screen. I managed to answer the call.

'Where are you?' Elli shouted down the phone over the music at her end. 'We're going back soon. Although, if we do, it means this lot have won the bet and they'll be out later than us.'

I managed to breathe the word *okay*, before she was telling me I sounded funny. Nico was holding my free hand in his and kissing my wrist. I agreed to come back to the bar and hung up the phone.

'Elli says they're going back to the apartment—' Before I could finish, he lightly kissed my lips.

'We best go then.' His smile was slightly crooked and gorgeous. He turned to pick up the things he had tossed to the ground but I noticed his eyes dart about and his body language shift. His fingers were aggressively running through his hair then through the sand.

'What's wrong?' I stood and looked down at the dark shapes on the ground, finding it hard to make out what was what.

'My keys. They are gone.'

We both dropped to our hands and knees to feel about in the sand. We had no luck. Nico was absolutely freaking out. I did my best to reassure him. Eventually he decided he should walk me back to the bar then come back and keep looking alone. If he didn't find them, he would sleep on the beach. I protested but he started walking and there was nothing I could do other than follow him, kicking up sand to catch up.

A Key

As soon as we were back with my friends, I explained that Nico had dropped his keys and we should not let him sleep on the beach; that he would have to stay with us in the apartment. Nico was determined not to put us out, but I was equally determined he was staying with us. Luckily, my girls felt the same way as me, and we all dragged him back to our apartment.

We laid down bedding on the cool tiles for him to sleep on. If I'm honest, the beach would have probably been more comfortable, but I still felt happier knowing he was with us. We were all in one large room together, and it wasn't long until sleep crept in. Not for me though. After a while, I sat up in my bed to look at the floor where Nico was. The bathroom door had been left ajar, leaving a warm glow to stream in from a lamp outside. I could make out that his eyes were wide open.

'Are you awake?' I hissed, knowing full well that he was either awake or slept with his eyes open. His eyes sharply turned to face me and he brought himself up onto his elbow.

'No. You?' Light glanced over his top lip as he smiled.

I shook my head, giggling silently from my bed. Although it was a single bed, there was room enough for the two of us. I shuffled over and tapped the empty space next to me. He shook his head. In response, I tilted mine and whispered, 'If you don't, then I'll sleep on the floor.'

At that, he shook his head once more, his chin lowering, but he got up in spite of himself and lay next to me in the bed.

Nothing happened. Nothing was said. I just nestled down in his arms and we both fell fast asleep.

When I woke up, Nico wasn't next to me and I could hear voices on the balcony. Looking up, I could see Lottie was asleep with her hair looking like someone had back-combed it over her face. Lightly, I edged close to the balcony but not close enough to be seen. Peeking my head around, I could see Nico with his arms firmly around Elli. The image stung like a wasp's venom sticking in my throat, making it swell. I darted back behind the curtain like a child as they released from their embrace.

'What are you doing?' My heart bounced inside my chest as guilt rolled along my skin in waves of goosebumps. Lottie was croaking at me and sitting up. I laughed as casually as I could, and muttered some nonsensical words before braving the heat out on the balcony.

'Good morning.' I was going for casual and bright but I edged towards shrill. Nico stepped towards me and bent forwards to kiss me. At the last moment, I instinctively turned my face so he only caught the side of my lips. I was too confused to let him kiss me. His eyes flicked between mine, scanning my face before pulling me out a white plastic chair.

'It's not a good morning,' Elli said and slumped down into her chair. That's when I noticed her puffy eyes and the slightly blotchy, pink edges to her skin.

'What's happened?' All thoughts of Nico were tipped off the edge of the balcony as Elli's chest did a juddered inhale. Lottie bellowed something about coffee from inside, but I just snapped a *no* and nodded for Elli to continue.

'Oh, I'm being dramatic. I didn't even know her, not really. This girl from uni committed suicide. It's just so dreadful. I'm being silly.' Elli looked down at her phone then pressed it over her mouth. A new tear slipped down her cheek as she spoke behind her phone. 'Someone put RIP on Facebook with her photo. Sorry, I don't mean to be a downer – it's just a shock.'

Lottie appeared interrupting with more coffee questions. Soon, she had her arms around Elli, who recited what she had just said to me. We lavished reassurance on her as best we could. She was quiet though, more than I would expect for a loss of someone she didn't really know. But, these things sometimes just catch. The loss of a life, especially someone so young, is a shock.

'I have to be going.' Nico edged in between our conversation, then pulled his keys from his pocket.

Lottie and I both spoke at once, asking questions and spitting words of confusion.

'I went down to the beatz early. They were under the sunbed.' A small smile lifted my face, enjoying his Greek accent and the way he said beach. He was rolling his eyes at the situation, relief was present in the smile that crossed his lips. I persuaded him to wait for me to get dressed so I could walk him to his bike.

As soon as we were out of the apartment, he was asking me if I was okay. I had to come clean and tell him I saw the embrace with Elli. He made a sarcastic little tutting sound.

'You were not jealous? No? Of my arms around Elli? Poor Alice.' He pulled me to a stop and wrapped his arms around my waist. 'Now they are yours.' He looked down at me, and without a thought, I kissed him. I wanted him to be mine and mine alone. I thought about Maria and Harry. Could I do that?

Drop everything and move to Corfu? Maybe Nico would be interested in England? I had goals after all and I couldn't put all of that on hold. I was doing well at uni, getting top marks in every project I had undertaken. I was studying something I was passionate about: the planet and the environment. My ambitions were to improve things for everyone walking this earth and I couldn't reject all that, however much I liked someone. It was bigger than me and what I wanted.

We arrived at Nico's bike and he didn't want me walking back on my own, so he gave me a lift back to the apartment before a last kiss goodbye.

Calm

I didn't want to make the rest of the holiday about Nico and me. Of course, I did want that, but I knew I shouldn't and there was no way I would. Elli had really closed down since finding out about the girl's suicide. She said she was fine, but she was too quiet. If the subject was broached, she wouldn't open up about it anymore than she already had. Lottie and I put it down to shock and did our best to keep her smiling. It meant pushing my thoughts and desires to one side.

Nico and I texted each other though, but I didn't spend any real time with him for two days. One of those nights he was working, but I only got to wave at him in passing. The bar he worked in was heaving and there was nowhere to sit. So, instead, we went to another bar with our fifty-something counterparts that night.

Early the next morning, I was up and the girls were sleeping. I messaged Nico to see what he was doing, and if he could get to me for coffee. There were no questions. He said he was on his way.

An hour passed with no more messages and no sign of him. The girls were still sleeping and I was beginning to get anxious. I checked on my phone and it said Sidari to Agios Stefanos was only around fifteen minutes by car or bike. Another grating ten minutes passed by before I heard a bike coming along. I left a note for my friends on the dressing table and crept out to meet Nico.

He was apologising before his open-face helmet was fully off his head.

'I was beginning to worry.' I suspected he could read it on my face. I don't really think I had to tell him. He looked drained, as though he hadn't slept all night. 'What's happened?'

'My brother. He was having bad sleeps, bad dreams,' he said, correcting himself. His accent was heavier, just like his tired eyelids. 'Kostas is still big, strong. I have to help. My father had to be out working.' His voice was low, almost amounting to no more than a vibration in his chest. I reassured him that I understood. Of course, I couldn't truly understand how hard it was, only that it made him late and sometimes put his life off track. I admired him. Even though it was only a matter of days being around him, I honestly felt proud to know him, proud of his sacrifice, and hurt for the pain that cut him so deeply.

I took his soft, clean-shaven face in my hands and kissed him. He pulled me in, our bodies pressing tightly together. We kissed fervently, deeply, and I wished I could have stayed in that kiss forever. I still wish that.

A voice called something in Greek. It was an older gentleman walking along the other side of the road. We pulled apart. Nico laughed and said something back. The old man shrugged and laughed before carrying on. I asked what he had said, but Nico just laughed and shook his head. I pushed him a little until he happily told me the old man had said I was much too good for him and that he had agreed.

Instead of coffee, we went to a place called Silver Star where I had a milkshake, although Nico had coffee to perk himself up a little. As we sipped, I asked more about what his brother was like before the accident. It quickly became clear how close the two boys had been, getting into scrapes together, Nico wanting to be just like him but always feeling like he was falling short of the charm and talent of his brother.

I thought he was plenty charming enough. Although he did enjoy putting on a flirtatious act at times, it could feel a bit put on. I was quite sure he had gained it from looking up to Kostas and his way with women. Although he did also admit it had already helped him to get some tips while working at the bar.

As we were talking, my phone vibrated in the pocket of my dress. I pulled it out, as I was sure it would be Elli or Lottie checking up on me. It wasn't. It was Ethan. Ethan. His name there on my screen made me feel almost faint. He had only messaged me once before. He had got my number from a mutual friend and asked if I could move my car one time. I could see the beginning of the message he had just sent:

Yo, how's it going? I heard you were in Corfu. When ...

That was all I could see without opening the message. Why was he sending me a message now?

'What is wrong?' I looked up to be presented with Nico's worried expression, his body starting to lean in towards me. It was stupid, but I didn't want to tell him it was the boy I had fancied at home. I claimed it was nothing and tucked the phone back in my pocket before picking up my strawberry milkshake and attempting to drown myself in it.

'Can I take you somewhere today? I know you're here with your friends, but I want to know you more. I don't have work today as I am still on a trial.'

51

With the message from Ethan lingering in my pocket, I didn't know what to say. Elli and Lottie were probably just going to sleep things off on the beach anyway, but I didn't want to come on holiday and just ditch them. I sent a voice message to our group chat asking if it would be alright. Within minutes I got one back from Elli:

Of course, crazy girl! Just be safe and be back for dinner. Lovey-love-kiss!

All I could hear was Lottie sniggering in the background at Elli's sarcasm and poorly put-on Greek accent. I had to laugh too, but I'm sure my cheeks flushed as Nico listened to the message along with me.

'It's a yes. Where are we going and what do I need?'

'First, let's borrow a helmet.'

Soon we were on his bike, meandering along the dusty roads, absorbing the views of pure, light-blue skies and the undulating carpet of olive groves and pointed cypress trees. It was idyllic. Perfect. The air rushing past my skin cooling it against the intense heat of the sun piling down on us; Nico's firm body under my palms. Perfect. Nico said he would take me for a ride and stop for lunch. I had no idea where we were going, or even what direction we were going in. I'd never felt freer than when I was with him. As though I could do anything, be anything. There was nothing holding me back. No measuring stick to tell me if I was achieving enough or working hard enough. There was just calm.

I think starting out by not liking him much helped free up my mind. He wasn't on a pedestal. He was just Nico. Not like Ethan, who I'd lifted above anyone else within my imagination.

Ethan. The thought of him tinged my cheeks red with guilt. I still hadn't opened his message. Part of me never wanted to; the other part was worried he might have had something important to say. The question in my mind thrust me out of my relaxed, free moment and into a world of unknown. A world divided by the here and now and the unknown entity that was the future.

As my mind went along its own road, Nico took us up high, passed scorched, golden grasses and dark green hills. Our journey ended in a small village. It was tiny, in fact, with a scattering of houses with higgledy-piggledy bricks of beige and white. We passed a tall, terracotta belfry and a couple of chickens clucked past us, feathers puffing and ruffling at the noise of the motorbike.

We came to a stop outside the one eatery. It was a simple space: a flat roof over an open terrace scattered with wooden tables and chairs of different shapes and sizes. Nico was warmly welcomed by a gentleman, perhaps in his fifties. The impression I had was that they knew each other well. This was soon confirmed to me as it was revealed he was Nico's mother's cousin. He welcomed me too, in a mixture of Greek and broken English.

To the echoing sound of cicadas, we took our place at a wooden table with worn dark chairs, and waited as it was all carefully laid with a paper cloth and knives and forks tightly wrapped in napkins. Nico chatted to the man softly while he worked. I was sure there was a look from the man in my direction, perhaps a question or a compliment. Nico beamed at me, sitting tall in his chair, before reaching his hand across the table to take mine.

'This place is beautiful. Where are we?' I asked once we were alone.

'Corfu.' Nico grinned, but didn't look up from his menu. 'I told you. All is nice here.'

'I believe you.' Somewhere in the deepest part of my being, that sense of calm rolled over me again, and encased me in a bubble of cicada chants, like a baby, peaceful in its mother's womb.

We ordered our food. I say we, but in fact I told Nico I'd like a Greek salad with freshly squeezed orange juice and he ordered it before lounging back in his chair, fingers knotting behind his head, showing all the definition of his lean muscles. A sweet smell rolled over from some pretty red flowers to the side of the taverna and all was sweet. All was calm. All was nice.

Nothing of note happened there, up on that hill or mountain or wherever we were. There, in Corfu, where everything is nice. I remember lingering kisses and holding hands, and the feel of Nico brushing my auburn hair from my eyes, and the sweet taste of him on my lips. But, I can't remember what we talked about or how he managed to make me feel so strongly for him. What could possibly have been said to have brought me to where I am now? I couldn't remember anything specific about that lunch, other than how it left me. It left me yearning to stay there. Right there in that very spot. I could have happily stayed with Nico chatting to me, gently laughing along with me. Perhaps telling stories of our lives up to that point, or dreaming about the future. Whenever I think about that lunch, it's like the golden glow of the sun trickled down on us and gave us its embers to burn in our souls. But that's the thing about fire. It burns. It glows too hot and it has the potential to swallow everything up.

And that's what happened. The switch that living brings. The balance of good and bad. We were just deciding whether to order another drink when Nico's phone rang. The conversation was quick and his entire being changed. The contented lift of his cheekbones died and the scar of pain resonated on his forehead instead.

Kostas

'That was my mother. She needs help with Kostas. I must get to them now. Will you come with me?' He was already standing, gathering his things, shouting goodbye to the owner, his mother's cousin, and I was just trailing behind, bewildered. Of course I agreed to go. What choice did I have anyway? Say no? Make him take me back to my beach life before letting him help his mother in the reality of his life? No. Of course not. An edge of nerves bit into my belly, wondering what his brother was truly like, how bad he might be, but I wanted to help in any way I could.

He made his bike go a little faster on the way back. Not dangerously so, but I could feel the tension in his body echo out into mine as we were pressed together. The trees nipped by in more of a blur, but the journey seemed to take twice as long. Not that it did, of course. It's just the funny perception of time when there's a panic in the air. In rushing about, everything seems to take forever.

As houses started to more densely fill the lanes, we pulled up outside a sunshine-yellow house that was set back from the road. We dismounted, pulling our helmets off. I was smoothing my hair, trying to regain a level of presentable to meet his mother, when he ordered me to wait by the bike.

'No. I didn't come to just wait outside like a dog.'

This caught Nico off-guard. He had already started to walk towards the front door. He turned back, shaking his head.

'No, no. I don't know what has happened. You must stay here.'

'No, you might need me. I'm not staying outside.' I grabbed his hand and held it tightly between my fingers. He looked up to the sky and muttered something in Greek before agreeing. I think he only agreed because he didn't want a moment's more delay.

As we walked in the door, he was calling for his mother. I followed him as we weaved our way past ornaments, mirrors and pale-yellow walls lined with family photos. All before the accident. They must have been. Kostas looked like a bulkier version of Nico with longer hair, wavy and down to his shoulders.

A voice called back to Nico from upstairs. He started jogging, with me only one step behind. He called out, a burst of more words. The only one I understood was my name. I assumed preparing his mother for me, an unexpected visitor in their family home.

As we arrived in front of his mother, he took her square face in his hand and bent to kiss her cheek before more words were spoken at a pace I could never replicate – if I understood them or not – before Nico darted along the corridor to gently knock on a door. He started speaking in a soft and melodic voice to talk to Kostas through the door.

That was when his mother's attention was turned on me. A strained-but-warm smile lifted her face. The day had obviously been a tough one and it was only early afternoon.

'Alice, I am Lyra, Nico's mother.' Her English was very

good, although she spoke slowly, as though each word had a measurement it had to fulfil. 'I am sorry to meet you like this. Please forgive me.'

I did my best to reassure her and to offer any assistance that was needed. She explained that Kostas had become unsettled when she needed him to stop what he was doing and wash up for lunch. It had escalated. He had pushed her away then gone to his bedroom. There was no lock on the door but she couldn't get in. He was still strong and had moved his furniture to prevent her entry. She called Nico, knowing it was his day off, so her husband wouldn't have to be called away from work. Lyra told us she was worried he had hurt himself because he started crying about his finger and calling for her help but she couldn't get in.

After ten minutes of cooing and coaching, Nico still had no luck. He decided he was going to have to get a ladder and force his way in that way. Running to the next house along, he managed to borrow one that was almost tall enough, but not quite. With more calm conversation, Kostas opened the window. There was child-proofing in the window, of sorts, but Nico managed to just about manoeuvre his fingers to open it fully and climb in to get the door open.

'Kostas will be happy to meet you. Your pretty face will help to calm him down,' Lyra informed me.

She was right. But there was a bigger issue. When we followed Nico into the room, it was soon apparent that Kostas had smashed a snow globe and badly cut his finger. His face was red and puffy from crying and his bed was soaking in blood. He wailed and cuddled his mother before seeing me. As soon as he saw me, he wanted to touch my auburn hair and chatted away at me in Greek, tears rolling down his cheeks as he showed me his finger.

Blood was quickly matted into my hair as no one could persuade him to stop. His bad finger was still being pressed to his chest, of course, but the good hand was covered in blood from holding the cut one.

I caught sight of Nico. He had been busy putting wooden furniture covered in stickers back in its place, but he kept watching Kostas and me interact from the corner of his eye. Nico's jaw was clenched tightly shut, as though he had been wired that way. He didn't stop and he didn't say anything.

Kostas was just like a child in personality. Even though I couldn't understand his words, his body language was easily read. His wide eyes danced in wonderment at me. When he grinned in anticipation of responses I couldn't give, from complete lack of understanding, I noticed two of his front teeth were missing. It must have happened during the accident as he had teeth in all the photos downstairs.

Behind our little exchange, Nico and Lyra began talking, organising, debating and almost arguing. I tried to talk to Kostas. Even if it was two conversations with no relevance to each other, he seemed to prefer when I spoke back and when I showed him pity for his hurt finger, or smiled at the cartoon on his T-shirt.

'I need your help. It has been decided that my mother will take Kostas to the hospital to have his finger looked at. I need you to lead him to the car. He is interested in you; he will follow you with ease.'

So, I chatted to him. The once big-and-handsome man, and now the vulnerable child. I took his good hand and let him follow me down the stairs, out to the car, where I strapped him in and gave him a kiss on the cheek to say goodbye. Not that he understood, but I told him to be better and that I hoped we would meet again soon. Lyra thanked me, repeatedly, before driving away to the hospital in Corfu Town.

'You need a shower'—Nico paused—'and new clothes.' I looked down at the drips of blood on my black-and-white striped dress and the matted patch of hair where Kostas had twisted it around with his bloody fingertips.

Nico didn't have much to say as we went back in the house. There was no added charm or flirtation, and the quiet in the house was like a wall between us. I followed him back up the stairs, where he pulled a towel from the airing cupboard and led me to a small bathroom with a shower over the bath.

'Let me take your dress. I will wash it and find you some clothes.' He held out his hand but I hesitated.

'Wait, on a normal wash, blood might not come out. It needs to be cleaned in cold water first.' Taking my phone and purse from my pockets, I pulled the dress over my head and turned on the tap. Standing in my underwear, I rinsed out the blood as best I could, before turning back and passing it to him. It was then that I noticed the little smile on his face. 'Well, I'm glad I got you smiling again.'

A light chuckle resonated from him before I stepped forwards and gently pressed my lips to his. Then he left me alone to clean the mess from my hair.

When I came back out, Nico was walking down the stairs with all his brother's bedding in his arms. He told me to go in the room to my left and he would be back soon. It was his bedroom. A single bed with white walls and black-and-white bedding. It was all simple furnishings with a frameless mirror above a set of plain wooden drawers that were scattered with aftershaves and lotions.

The room had a fan on the ceiling and I pulled the chain to start it whirling. Sweat was already threatening on my skin even after a cool shower. If the house had air-con, it wasn't everywhere and I don't know that it was on. I was already dry, so I placed my underwear back on and went in search of some clothes in Nico's drawers. I pulled out a black T-shirt with some Greek writing on it, and a pair of charcoal shorts that would fall right off if I didn't hold them up. It was enough to sit on the bed and look passably presentable though.

I continued to squeeze my hair in fists between the fibres of the soft white towel, but the heat was working well enough to dry it. I perched on Nico's unmade bed, scanning the room while I waited. He clearly hadn't been expecting company, as the room was littered with clothes, game remotes, headphones and other random items. As he walked in, I think he had already picked up on my line of thought.

'Sorry, sorry. I didn't think you would be coming here.' He started bundling clothes into drawers when he caught sight of me and started to laugh. 'I like your outfit. Do you know what that means?' He pointed at the words across my chest and I shook my head in response, looking down, wondering what they could mean. 'My brother bought this one for me. I won't tell you what it says, only that he used to find himself very funny. Not like he is now. Watching him and you, it makes me so sad, so angry. He used to have all the charm, a beautiful girlfriend.' He momentarily paused in his tidying and looked up to the ceiling. I couldn't be sure, but I thought he was balancing tears in his eyes, tilting his head back to hold them in place before continuing. 'She comes to visit sometimes, with pity all on her eyes. If this had not happened to him …'

He didn't finish the sentence and I didn't push him to. Words weren't required. My whole body ached at the sight of his pain. I watched him as he silently continued tidying, his words about his brother hanging in the air, whirling around my head along with the air from the fan. It made it all more real to see him in his home and get a gauge of how things really were for him. He obviously still had a strong bond with his brother, but not in the way it was. Not in the way it should be.

A Single Bed

When the room was more presentable, Nico lay himself on the bed next to me knotting his fingers behind his head again. Lunch already felt like days ago, not hours. Instinctively, I placed myself next to him, wrapping in around him for comfort. He looked down at me, his face tense as though he was holding in words that were ready to fall out if he wasn't careful about it.

'I like you, Alice.'

'I like you too.'

'Crazy girl,' he laughed and I playfully slapped his firm torso.

'Shut up. I'm not crazy.'

'You are to like me.'

'Don't say that. I think you're incredible, the way you are with Kostas and your mum … most of the men I know wouldn't do all you're doing for your family.'

He was very still for a time before replying. 'Then they are not men. Maybe they are not human.'

'Well, I think any girl would be very lucky to have you.'

'Yes?' He shifted his weight to face me. 'I know which girl I want to be lucky.' The smirk on his face made me instantly giggle, but before I could make any more comment on the matter, his lips found mine and a hint of tobacco filled my mouth as his tongue roamed freely with mine. As his hands slipped up my T-shirt, he laughed again. 'I've never undressed a girl wearing my clothes before,' he chuckled before lifting it over my head. We carefully helped each other to shed clothes; that exterior layer that we all use to protect us and define us. Then that's all there was: us. My porcelain skin pressed to his dark olive tones, our fingers exploring each other's bodies, our mouths finding every curve, every tender spot to be devoured.

We were there on his bed with the humming sound of the fan over our heads for a long time, so much time that I questioned how long we could possibly stay alone, uninterrupted. He reassured me, knowing it would be a long time before anyone would be home again.

I don't think I'd have been able to stop myself either way. I wanted to be with him. If we only had minutes or we had a lifetime. I just wanted to be with him. To feel him inside me and to keep him there for as long as I could. The urge to hold him and protect him and be with him had become all-consuming in the heat of the Corfu sun.

So there on his single bed, he made love to me. It's not a phrase I use lightly. But looking back, I know that's what it was. He held on to my body and looked at my face, kissed my neck, caressed me until we both released all the tension we had been balling up together. We were practically strangers and yet I felt closer to him than any boyfriend I'd ever had.

For a long time after, we held each other in silence. I think we were both afraid to break the trance as we knew he would then have to take me back to my friends. It was only broken when his phone started ringing. I cursed phones as an invention, always there to interrupt every solitary, beautiful moment. It was his mother again, this time to say she had called Nico's father and he was meeting her at the hospital. They were going to stay at her brother's house that night. It was near to the hospital and Kostas was being very difficult with the staff so it was going to be a late one. They would be back in the morning. As soon as he replaced his phone on the pine bedside table, his eyes were on mine.

'Stay,' he said. It was closer to a demand than a question. The tone of his voice was threadlike and it reeled me in. Without another thought, I had agreed and was leaving a message with my friends, hoping they would forgive me for putting myself first. They did of course. That's what good friends do.

'Do you seduce all the tourists?' I whispered into his ear before nibbling his soft lobe between my lips.

'No'—he lifted one side of his mouth into a smile—'you are my first tourist.'

'I'm sure I won't be the last,' I said, lying on my back to watch the fan rotating above me. Nico lifted his weight onto his elbow to look over me, his fingertips tracing a line from my hip bone along to my nipple.

'I hope you are,' he whispered, before his tongue lightly flicked along my nipple, making a quiet hum rise out of my chest.

'Me too.' I shouldn't have said it. I should have never gone in that house. I should have stayed outside, kept my distance. I should never have stayed the night, or given myself to him the way I did, because the longer I was with him, the more I wanted him to keep. That burning ember scarred me with every embrace, left him deep inside me in a way that could never be removed, and I never wanted to leave.

We stayed up most of the night, talking, holding each other, fusing together our soft skin and consuming all our energy just to watch the pleasure on the other one's face for as long as we could.

One Corfu Summer?

The girls ribbed me. I am useless at keeping anything from them, so I told them everything in its entirety. Every detail of it. They were both a little shell-shocked by the whole thing. I don't think they pegged me for a holiday romance-type. I'd never done anything quite like it before and I couldn't rationalise it either.

'I have one question,' Elli began, 'what did the message from Ethan actually say?'

I'd said about the message in passing at the start of my lengthy tale but that was what Elli had taken from it all, that missing piece of information.

'I don't know. I haven't opened it yet.'

'Come on, little miss lovey-love-kiss. I know that Nico has spilled his Greek magic all over you, but aren't you a little interested in Ethan?' Lottie said, before putting a fork full of a tomatoey Greek stew called *stifado* in her mouth.

I think I was afraid to open it. To find out anything that could push me away from the bubble I'd created in Corfu. I picked up my phone from the table and went to the message and began to read. '*Yo—*'

'Oh god, who starts a message with *Yo?*' Lottie spluttered through a mouthful of stew but was quickly shushed by Elli who wanted me to continue. I started again:

'Yo, how's it going? I heard you were in Corfu? When are you back? Do you fancy meeting up over the summer? I'll be staying with my dad in Colchester and I don't know anyone around there. It would be nice for a friendly face to show me around.'

I looked up from my phone to see both of my friends opposite with their knives and forks tightly pressed between their fingers, hanging on to my every word.

'What are you going to do?' Elli's voice came out like a shadow, almost transparent and inaudible above the music in the taverna. I shrugged. I wasn't sure what to say. I wanted to stay there in Corfu with Nico.

'Tell him yes!' Lottie snapped, looking from Elli to me. 'Nico is a dream, Alice. What are you going to do? Quit uni?'

'No.' I was doing well at uni and environmental issues were something I was passionate about. I knew I couldn't quit. Not for anyone.

'Exactly. Nico is just a cute bit of holiday fun and Ethan is real. He goes to your uni, he wants to meet up, and you've fancied him for a year! How is there even a question?' Lottie went back to putting stew in her mouth, giving Elli just enough time to add her ideas into the melting pot.

'But look at Harry and Maria. He gave up everything because he knew he loved her. Nothing is off limits when it comes to love.' Elli was being sweet but something in her words was more painful than Lottie's pragmatism. Did I love him? Could I love him? I wasn't quite twenty. How was I meant to know the difference between love and lust? I didn't feel like I had the necessary skill set to pick the two apart after only a week with Nico.

'That's the difference, Elli. They are in love. Do you love

Nico?' Lottie poked her fork at me.

'No!' I snapped, but I still wasn't sure. If the answer was yes, I wasn't ready to admit it to myself let alone my friends. My feelings for him were overwhelming, that much I knew. I wanted to be with him, in his presence.

'Well then. There's your answer. Text Ethan and say you'll meet up when you're back.'

That much I could do. No matter what happened, I knew eventually I would return, so saying I would see him when I was back didn't feel dishonest. Only, I didn't anticipate his response:

Good. I keep thinking about our chat the other night. You're good to talk to. How's Corfu?

I didn't want to strike up a full conversation but I didn't want to shut him down either. Everything was muddled in my mind and all I really wanted was to close my eyes and wake up back in Nico's single bed with his naked body pressed to mine and his arms locking me to him. It wasn't going to happen. Instead, a message from him appeared next to the one from Ethan:

I keep thinking about you. When can I see you again?

I just wanted to hide in one of the coves around the beach and drown there. Instead, I let my friends chew over what I could do, and what I should do, as they compared and contrasted my situation to experiences of their own, like it was a science project. None of it was useful. None of it helped the dull ache that was throbbing in my chest.

I couldn't bring myself to return either message that night. I went to bed thinking about them both. I wanted Nico. It was typical that this would be the moment Ethan showed a passing interest in me. The bigger problem was Lottie was right. Where could this go? I had a life in England and none of it included moving to Corfu. It wasn't as though I could see Nico leaving his family either. He might move out of the family home, but there was no way he would abandon them when they so heavily relied on him. I may have only known him for a few days but that was something I was sure of.

We only had one more day left in Corfu. That was it. What was the point in doing this to myself? I needed to reply to him but I didn't know what to say. Sitting up to grab my phone, I thought of him lying on the floor on the night he lost his keys. How he had got in my bed and held me. Sleeping next to him was the best I'd slept in a long time. Would I ever sleep like that again?

In the dim light I wrote out a message to him:

We leave tomorrow night. Can I see you in the afternoon, to say goodbye? xxx

Even though it was the middle of the night, his reply was instant and he sent a time and a place to meet.

We hadn't paid the extra for the air-con, so when the tears started to trickle down my face, they were almost cool against my prickling skin. Every part of me didn't want to let go of him. But I knew I would have to.

On our last day, we lounged around the pool and I could feel the girls were trying extra hard to be fun or funny. I smiled and laughed in all the right places but my heart wasn't in it. I'd left it there in Nico's bed.

I put on my favourite dress that afternoon. It was covered in pale-pink roses and made me feel like perhaps he would sweep me off my feet and there would be a way we could make things work. I waited for him. But he didn't show up. There was no message with an explanation and nothing I could do.

I got on the coach that night, broken that I didn't get to say goodbye to him and that he hadn't even bothered to turn up or message me. Maybe I was just another tourist to him? Maybe he had feigned care for his brother to seduce women into thinking he had a good heart? He had ghosted me. Just like Tess had done to Lottie. I pinched at my hands to focus away from my desire to cry, my abdomen like marble, stopping my breathing from spluttering out tears.

Just as the airport was in sight through the window on the coach, a message vibrated on my phone. It was Nico:

Are you here still? Kostas took my phone. He was having very bad day. I could not leave him. He is sleeping now. Can I see you? Please. X

Me:

It's too late, I'm at the airport. If things were different, I think I could have loved you. Be safe, and I wish you the best life here on Corfu, where everything is nice. xxx

Nico:

I understand. You have a life without me. I want you to know. For me, I don't think I could have loved you. I know I love you. You know where to find me.

I left Corfu to return to Ethan. But Nico had left his fingerprints on my heart. And that was something I would never recover from.

About the Author

Catlow loves travel. Born and brought up in the heart of Suffolk, Catlow has travelled extensively in Europe with her French husband and, more recently, their two young children. Of all the places she's been it is the Greek islands that have captured her heart. She visits as often as family commitments allow.

The Little Blue Door is Catlow's first novel – written during the lockdown of 2020 while feeding her baby in the early hours. She has previously written plays alongside being a lyricist and performer.

To stay up to date go to www.FrancescaCatlow.co.uk

You can connect with me on:
- https://francescacatlow.co.uk
- https://twitter.com/francescacatlow
- https://www.facebook.com/francescacatlowofficial
- https://www.instagram.com/francescacatlowofficial
- https://www.tiktok.com/@francescacatlow

Also by Francesca Catlow

The Little Blue Door 2021
Can a lost past lead to a beautiful future?

Melodie feels lost and alone, desperate to find something to remind her of her life before the pandemic. She sets out on a trip to Corfu to reconnect with happier times, only to be haunted by memories and events from the past.

While travelling, Melodie meets a handsome man with an intriguing young daughter. But Melodie doesn't want a holiday fling. It's not in her nature. After deciding to avoid the intriguing pair, their paths collide once more. But who holds the key to Melodie's past, and who will open the door to her future?

The Little Blue Door is the first in a trilogy of contemporary women's fiction and family saga. If you like raw emotions and a sexy slow burn romance set to the beautiful backdrop of Greece, then it's time to fly off to Corfu with Francesca Catlow's *Little Blue Door* series.

Read *The Little Blue Door* now to discover the secrets of Melodie's past and if she'll ever find the future she deserves.

Behind The Olive Trees 2022
She thought she'd found her lost past, but did she uncover all the secrets?

Chasing Greek Dreams 2023
She found her past, did it cost her future?

For His Love of Corfu: A Novella
A teenage decision can change everything.

Anton Greenwood is half English and half Greek, happily living on the island of Corfu. That is until his parents decide they want to expand their sons' horizons.

Can he make it on his own, or will he get in line with his family?

This *coming of age* story follows the popular character, Anton, from the 'Little Blue Door' series.

.

Printed in Great Britain
by Amazon